# Tales
# From
# Swankville

# Tales
# From
# Swankville

The Town May Be Fictional
But The Problem Is For Real

S.B. Fried with
Georgie H. Ikuma

**To order additional copies of this book, contact:**
Xlibris Corporation
1-888-795-4274
www.Xlibris.com
Orders@Xlibris.com
100255

# CONTENTS

To my editor and very special friend Georgeann Ikuma. Well, if meeting you at dance isn't fate, then I don't know what is. You are amazing. You are truly the least-competitive mom that I've ever met, and yet your daughter soars in those competitions. She truly shines on stage, and I honestly believe it's because she is up there because she wants to be there. You, my friend, have got that gentle push down without the great big, bad shove. I love to watch how you do it. You are wonderful, and I am so happy to call you a friend.

# A NOTE TO READERS

The essays on Swankvillains are inspired by situations that the authors have observed, heard, and sometimes participated in around their suburban towns. However, *Tales from Swankville* is a work of fiction. None of the characters are real people. Names and characters are the product of the authors' imaginations.

Any resemblance to actual events or persons, living or dead, is coincidental. Although the essays are inspired by the authors' own experiences, all situations and characters are used fictitiously.

Quotes from students are real, but names and ages have been altered.

# ACKNOWLEDGEMENTS

I WANT TO THANK my husband and children for their constant encouragement, love, and bluntness. They inspire me every day with constructive criticism that is offered so sincerely and succinctly. I am lucky to be surrounded by such authenticity and love.

FF—Thank you for your strength, compassion, support, and steady love.

SEF—Thank you for your encouragement and calling me your *role model*. You are my role model, too, as I admire your inner strength and drive in all that you do. You absolutely dance from your soul and with all of your heart. Whether on stage or in our garage, you shine! You make me proud every day, especially when you were given student of the week and student of the day for being yourself and doing what was right instead of following the crowd. You are a born leader and a gorgeous girl inside and out.

AOF—Thank you for your daily quotes that you share with me and read with such passion. I love your fire and fervor in everything you do. From soccer to softball, no matter the season, you are bold, brilliant, and beautiful on every field. I love to watch you be a leader in every situation. Your leadership sense, compassionate heart, and confident demeanor make you seem older than your nine years.

MNF—Our little star. My true miracle. You are so very handsome and adorable. Your joyful personality fills me with wonderful delight. You are proof that no one should ever tell someone *no* to his or her dreams. I never gave up, no matter what doctors said. I knew you were meant to be. Our fight to have you is just another reminder of how your dad and I never give up on anything we believe in especially when we know in our hearts and feel it in our guts. It is true that you learn the most from hard times and failure because then you can appreciate the good in your life and enjoy the happy times so much more.

To Mom and Dad, thank you for your unconditional love even when I am outspoken—something your sweet daughter would never have been growing up.

To Aunt Beth and Uncle Jeff, thank you for your support always.

To my sister, thank you for always having my back even when we don't see eye to eye.

To all my amazing, genuine friends, and yes, there are actually a lot of you. I'd like to especially thank Tracy, Susan, Suzanne, Jennifer, Erika, Sandy, Rocio, Kirsten, Diana, Georgeann, Jilly, Kathy, Karen, Kathy, Yvette, Cheryl, Bridget, and Carrie. Though I've always had a lot of friends around me, I've used the term much too loosely. So I thank those of you who have been there for so many years and never changed the definition of what a true friend is. You've made me appreciate the meaning of true friendship and how rare it is. This is a lesson that I wish I had learned much earlier. But then again, without my loose definition of a *friend*, these tales may not have existed.

# FOREWORD

*Little League Dad Assaults Team Coach*

*Hockey Dad Found Guilty of Manslaughter*

*Parents, Coaches Brawl After Soccer Game,*
*Parent Injured After Spat With Pop Warner Coach*

·   *Youth Coach Faced Gun-Toting Parent*

My issue is NOT with the competitive sports, the coaches, or the organizations that run them. I sign my kids up for a variety of competitive sports including soccer, cheer, dance, and softball at their insistence because they want to participate at that level. I truly am thankful for the learning and growth opportunities that this level of play affords children today. My concern, however, is with the attitudes and actions that parents display in front of their own children as well as their peers.

The headlines above are extreme examples of where our generation of parents has crossed the line. Sportsmanship, respectfulness, and abiding by rules, has been taken over by bullying, rudeness, and committing crimes. Why? Because, we as parents, want our children to be the best no matter what—even if it kills them.

My intention when writing these stories was not in any way meant to discount the world of competitive sports for our youth. Instead, my wish is that we can improve them by behaving like civilized human beings while cheering our children on to greatness.

# PART I

# ONCE UPON A TIME, PUSH CAME TO SHOVE

THE FOLLOWING COLLECTION of essays embodies the notion of "parents behaving badly," and the toll that their bad behavior is taking on the people around them. Parents today are being driven by a sense of competitiveness that seems to be flourishing by overwhelming degrees. Academics, sports, extracurricular activities, physical appearance, and material possessions—nothing is off-limits!

Our parents' generation coined the term "keeping up with the Joneses." Today, parents have no interest in merely "keeping up"; we need to do better. And this time, by golly, we're dragging our kids across the finish line with us!

Oh. By the way, I'm Sasha. As a mother of three children and a high school guidance counselor, I am privy to the short- and long-term effects this is having on the younger generations whose parents have unwittingly turned the gentle push of encouragement into a full-on shoving match. The quotes before each chapter are from my students that show first-hand the stress this generation of children is under.

Competition is making parents lose perspective of their important role of giving the gentle, encouraging push to a child that allows them to succeed or perhaps fail, but try nonetheless. It has been lost and instead replaced by a need for many parents to have the child that is "the best," ultimately leading to unkind adults and self-destructive kids. Parents are upping the ante, and we're all in!

Writing these essays forced me to look in the mirror, check myself, and make some changes. As parents, we have a responsibility to hold ourselves accountable for the sake of our children. They are our mirrors. They reflect our behavior and show it back to us through their own actions. Likewise, we are their mirrors. They emulate our actions and our words. They model our behavior; the behavior we're telling them is the right behavior. More importantly, as their mirrors, they see in our eyes affirmation, appreciation, affection, and approval. Don't they?

As you read the following stories, I hope that you will be able to find the humor in human nature at its worst. Hopefully, in the process, you too will find the lessons to be as valuable as I have. They are undoubtedly universal in their theme and common to varying degrees in the lives of families across the nation.

Interestingly, this particular tome of parents behaving badly takes place in a lovely town among pretty people. The setting, dare I say, is rather "fairytale-esque."

Life never seemed hard to outsiders who see Swankville moms driving around in their BMWs and suburbans. My mother pushed me into every sport, dance class, and activity that all the other neighborhood girls were doing. I was the fat, quiet kid, and she hated that.

-Alisa

## CHAPTER 1

# Mirror, Mirror on the Wall, Who's the Swankiest of Them All?

*Snow White and Her Three Dwarfs*

"WHO *IS* THE Swankiest of them all?" This is the question that floats through my head as I add a streak of liner across my eyelid in preparation for another day in Swankville. You may be familiar with this fairytale town. It's home to the beautifully tree-lined streets, SUVs on steroids, politically correct Priuses, and competitive parents, otherwise and affectionately known as Swankvillains.

Slipping into my nice workout gear, I listen to my three kids chattering away downstairs and feel a twinge of guilt that I'm allowing them to fend for themselves while I take a little extra time to look nice just to take them to school.

My middle child Carter bursts through the bedroom door.

"Mom, are you wearing *that* to drop us off at school? Why don't you wear necklaces and a little more makeup like Madison's mom?"

Mental note: At just nine years old, my daughter is aware of this! Before I can respond, she turns on her heel, races down the stairs, and calls out to remind me, "Don't forget to come to my class party today. All the other kids' moms will be there."

Well, good-bye guilt of thirty seconds ago, hello, new guilt!

After dropping my two girls off at school, I return home with my rough-and-tumble two-year-old boy, Jake, who immediately leads me to his dirt patch near our front lawn where he sits and digs for the next hour. I stretch out on the relaxing porch of our large remodeled home and begin to document my adventures in Swankville.

My son is happy and occupied, and I have a lot to write down. I smile to myself, enjoying my sense of peace and contentment as I reflect on the toddler days of my older children. If they were busy playing, I would rush to the phone to gossip with one of my fellow playgroupies. I recall that it didn't feel good or peaceful. I can see now that their friendship, which was rooted in gossip, served a function in an escapism sort of way—not in a "heals my soul" sort of way.

Big difference!

Those were the days when I first realized I needed to start looking in the mirror. I did look, and that's when I started to make some changes. Oh, don't get me wrong; I have my days when I slip up. And now, in addition to the mirrors in my bathroom, I've got three more around me all the time, and they each have a set of big blue eyes that stare back at me and remind me of the type of parent I want to be.

Later in the day, as I drive through the streets of Swankville, I look out my windows enjoying the lovely view my neighborhood has to offer. My gaze rests on the beautifully landscaped yards. I smile quietly to myself as I realize how less lovely some of these homes appear to me now that I know what they and their owners are like on the inside.

Sometimes there's not enough makeup in the world to paint a realistic facade—not even in Swankville.

It's not about how rich the people are in a town, but about parents' own insecurities. Their low self-esteem and intense parenting are hurting kids. It's time parents get back to basics and they realize that they as well as their kids are perfectly imperfect. With unconditional love and boundaries, everything can be worked on.

—Kelly

# CHAPTER 2

# What are Little Girls Made Of?

*Sugar and Spice, and Everything Nice,*
*Unless, of Course Her Friend Has Lice*

S O IN CASE I haven't made it clear, there are plenty of great reasons to live in Swankville—beautiful homes, expensive cars, fancy clothes—oh, and of course, the number one reason we all choose Swankville—the *best* schools. Because it's all about the children, right?

Every good fairytale, however, is tainted by an overbearing, evil entity—the wicked witch, the mean stepmother, the big bad wolf—you get the picture. As I've pointed out before, even Swankville is not immune to these unfriendly forces. For among the quaint cottages (read*: mansions*), the grassy knolls (read: *large, open parks*), and the cobblestoned paths (read: *wide, beautifully paved, tree-lined streets*), lurks the town's resident evil—the Swankvillains!

Today, to my utter dismay, I have discovered the one thing that can awaken a Swankvillain from its peaceful slumber quicker than a bullet out of a shotgun—a teeny, tiny, itsy, bitsy, smaller-than-the-tip-of-a-push-pin nit, otherwise known as *lice*!

The awakening of the Swankvillains began today when Carter came home from school. After dropping her backpack at the kitchen table, she joined me in the backyard to catch me up on another eventful day in third grade. Just as the warm sunshine was lulling me into a relaxed state, I let my gaze sweep over the golden strands of my daughter's beautiful hair. That's when I saw it.

I blinked hard twice, maybe three times, but I knew there was no batting it away.

Shining like the brightest star in the sky, like the blinding glare of the large headlights on my neighbor's shiny black Range Rover, was a white nit. It was the biggest, smallest thing I'd ever seen—Swankville's equivalent to the scarlet letter.

I know I have to do what is right.

First on my list is the walk of shame to confess, I mean report, the offending visitors to the school nurse's office. This is where the Swankvillains like to inconspicuously congregate in the morning to see who they need to shun that week.

Next are my dreaded phone calls to the parents and children who came to our house two days ago for a post-trick-or-treating sleepover on Halloween. They thought that night was scary; wait till they hear my news. This sure puts a new twist on the trendy tradition of "you've been booed." I might as well just concoct a poison-free hair potion and tack a note to each door that reads, "You've Been Liced."

After those two dreadful duties, spending the next forty-eight hours washing ten loads of laundry, ironing four complete bed sheets, and picking through three heads of hair no fewer than five times each, almost seems easy.

Sweaty, irritable, and physically exhausted, I'm relieved that the bugs have been extricated and that Carter can return to school.

Little do I know that a nit storm is a brewin'.

## What are Parents Made Of?—Kindness and Love, Good Things from Above, Until They Panic Over a Bug!

The nits may have met their demise, but the Swankvillain grapevine is ripe, bottled, and ready to be uncorked.

*Whine bottle number one* (full-bodied, with a not-too-subtle blend of self-centeredness and irritation)—Neurotic Nina, whose children are allergic to everything known to mankind, calls me for the first time ever to see if I can give her children a ride to school.

"Oh, Nina, any other day I would be more than happy to, but the lice service is coming to do a final check of the house."

The words fly out of my mouth before I can trap them in. It isn't just an honest mistake. It is, honestly, a big mistake!

She immediately panics and makes it all about her—her fears, her allergies, her neurosis. Listening to her, I yawn silently because, quite frankly at this point, I am feeling way more exhausted than exasperated.

During her first day back at school, Carter sees Nina and her daughter Jane. Clearly it didn't go well.

"Why did Jane's mom give her a lice treatment when Jane said she didn't have lice?" Carter asks.

I'm too bugged to comment.

*Whine bottle number two* (medium-bodied, with a not-too-subtle hint of overreaction)—Paranoid Paula, whose daughter Pia sits next to Carter in class, takes a page out of Nina's playbook.

At the end of Carter's second day back at school, Carter tells me that when she asked Pia where she was the day before, Pia said, "My mom kept me home because she heard someone in our class had lice."

I stare straight ahead and bite my tongue.

"She says her mother didn't give her the lice treatment, but I think she did because her hair was greasy," Carter continues. "It hurts my feelings that they are acting like that."

Again, I keep my mouth shut.

*Whine bottle number three* (robust with a slight detection of nuts and a bitter aftertaste)—The Annoyan's are the Swankvillains that provoke me into my own poor parental behavioral moment. Let's just say, this is when those pesky little nits manage to bite me in the butt!

Carter jumps into the car after basketball practice and bursts into tears. She has never done this, and I am visibly concerned.

"Pearl and Trina made fun of me tonight. They called me 'four eyes' and 'cheater,'" she manages between sobs. "They've been doing this all season." Just like a superhero from a Marvel comic book, I can physically feel my transformation into a "mama bear" taking place.

"Carter," I say, "you are an amazing basketball player and have done extraordinarily well all season. These girls are jealous, and the only way they know how to feel better about themselves is by putting you down."

"They are also saying 'Carter has lice' in a singsongy voice," she cries.

That did it! I sat down at the computer and began to compose an e-mail to the parents of the girls on the basketball team:

*Please remember that anyone can get lice and please remind your girls to be kind toward Carter.*

Then, in an admittedly weak moment, I actually identify some of the girls by name that were being mean. I press *send*.

Minutes later, seven to be exact, Pearl Annoyan's mother, Annie, calls me multiple times until I phone her back. She kept telling me, "That's not very nice to do to a nine-year-old."

After managing to get a word in edgewise, I ask her, "Can I please tell you the background?"

I explain how Carter was in tears after Monday's practice and that several girls, including hers, have teased her all season, and she has had enough. Now I hear that she's being taunted about lice, and when I sent out the e-mail, I did include some names out of frustration.

Annie said, "Well, you need to clear her name. I want you to apologize to all of them in an e-mail and copy me and my husband on it."

Let me get this straight, my daughter has been wronged, and now I'm being told to apologize to the parents of the daughter that was nasty to my child. The Annoyans' demands were not sitting well with me, and my argumentative tone was not sitting well with them.

My husband, who was phoned by Mr. Annoyan when I didn't respond to his wife's first four messages, calls on the other line to inform me I need to immediately rectify what is going on because he is on his way to present the biggest sales pitch of his career to the same company that Annie Annoyan works for, and he really wants the deal.

"WHAAAAAT!" I shriek with panic.

This is what my lapse in judgment has caused. All I'm doing is trying to raise the best kids I can. Annie's words hit me square in the face.

"You did this, Sasha."

In truth, I did. But what exactly did I do? Taking time to reflect in that big ol' shiny mirror, here is what I came up with. I tried to make my daughter feel better. I tried to protect her feelings from ever being hurt again. I fought a battle on her behalf. In doing so, perhaps I stepped in too soon as her superhero rather than giving her the tools—actions and words—to create her own armor and find strength during her own battles.

Maybe by trying to make her feel better, I was really trying to make myself feel better because, after all, when our children hurt, we hurt too. Probably, on some level, my exhaustion from dealing with the lice caused me to make a poor choice that could have lost my husband a wonderful job opportunity.

Through all this, the one thing I know I did do right is that I looked in the mirror and vowed to change my own behavior. I really don't believe Neurotic Nina, Paranoid Paula, or the Annoyans' realize yet how their actions and words ultimately affect the behavior of their own children. I do know, however, that I can only change myself.

Oh, and if the whole lice situation has put the fear of God in you, please don't worry. I mean, yes, the nits are an abominable force to be reckoned with, but I've yet to see the little critters win out over the chemical-free warfare designed by humans.

It's much more difficult dealing with the nitwits!

I overhear parents bragging at almost all my little brother's sporting events. I can only imagine how hard it must be to have to live up to those tough expectations. I think parents need to stop acting like their children are trophies or an award that shows how great of a parent they are.

—Joey

## CHAPTER 3

# Little Miss Muffet
# Sat on Her Tuffet
# Watching Soccer
# One Day
# Along came a Swankvillain
# Who, for Sure, was Not
# Chillin'
# And Chased Miss Muffet Away!

I STEP ONTO THE field and see a cacophony of kids kicking soccer balls around.

This should be a familiar scene as I've been to several soccer practices and games, but for some reason, it's different. This is a soccer tryout for Swankville's competitive league.

Swankville's kids can try out for competitive soccer at seven years old. So, when Carter was seven, after playing just one year of recreational soccer, her coaches and her dad (a baseball and soccer athlete) identified her as a naturally talented soccer player. Add that to the fact that she truly loves the sport and *voila!* Here I am keeping up with all the other intense parents who put their kids in competitive sports before they can even spell the word *competitive*.

I pause to survey the minefield of Swankvillains.

Most of them are intensely watching every play their daughters are making while others are quietly murmuring their predictions of which team each girl is going to be placed on. All of the kids' sport leagues in town try to be politically correct by labeling the teams with names of fruits, but I don't know whom they think they're fooling. The militant Swankvillains have decoded the rankings of Blueberries, Bananas, Strawberries, and Oranges, faster than I can say *fruit salad*.

I mean, honestly, I can practically see their calculating minds kick into algebraic overdrive.

- *Blueberries* are a super food, so obviously that's the best, hence, *team 1*.
- Then *team 2* is called *Bananas* because, of course, everyone is familiar with the term "second banana."
- Next, we have *Straw-ber-ries*. It has three syllables, so it's obviously *team 3*.
- And finally, *Oranges* is *team 4* because *or* rhymes with *four*, and well, there you have it.

So here I am taking my first foray into Swankville's soccer hysteria. I hold my baby Jake close to my chest in his Snuggie that I have strapped on like a suit of armor before going out to battle. I have just mere minutes to bask in my false sense of protection before I begin spotting the enemies.

To my right is the woman who scolded me for misspelling and mixing up her identical twin daughters' names at the Girl Scout party. I quickly recoil and turn to my left. Oops! Can't go that way. The Annoyans are holding court on the sidelines. I'd say, "Hello, how are you?" but I don't have time to write up an e-mail apology for it sounding like I said, "Mellow out you two."

I can't even walk straight ahead, or I'll get in the way of some very loving grandparents who yelled at me one time for blocking their view during a game.

Usually, I enjoy taking in my daughter's sporting events, but the intensity of these tryouts has literally sucked all the pleasure out of watching Carter kick around the soccer ball. Instead of chatting with each other, the parents are silently willing their daughters to be placed as high up on the fruit chain as possible.

After telling my husband, Eric, that I think he handles the negative energy surrounding competitive tryouts better than me, I make like a banana and split.

I played soccer for ten years, and at first, I loved it, but then it started to become less fun. I had a lot of pressure to make every practice and score every game to be considered as having had a good game. I think parents need to let children relax sometimes and play sports just for the pure enjoyment of the activity. If I wrote a book on the subject, I would title it, "Winners Do Not Always Have to Win!"

—Nate

# CHAPTER 4

# Mary, Mary Quite Contrary, How Did Your Team Do?

*Soccer Balls and Good Ref Calls,*
*We Won Ours by Two!*

LUKE RIDES HIS bike by my house each morning pulled by his three dogs as if he's Santa being ushered by his reindeer. Instead of shouting, "Merry Christmas to all," he hollers at me every Monday morning, "Did you win your game? We did, and Leeza scored two goals?"

He concludes his *SportsCenter* update before I've even had a chance to look up from shepherding my kids into the car.

One thing I do know is that Luke, like all Swankvillain soccer parents, has already checked the league's standings and not only knows where his own child's team ranks but that of his friends' and neighbors' teams as well.

As I saddle up my three kids for school, I think to myself, *I didn't win or lose the game.* In fact, I barely know the score since I spent the majority of the time chasing my toddler around the field while my daughter Carter was sidelined with an injury.

Luke's Monday morning quarterbacking really didn't start to bug me until about a month into his regular inquisition.

At first, I merely answered him; then as annoyance began to bubble my blood, I'd share how my preoccupations during the game take precedence over the actual outcome. Finally, when I reached my boiling point, I informed him that it's not about winning but doing your best and being a team player—even when you're injured.

Apparently, this fell on deaf ears.

The state cup tournament makes for an exciting weekend, but it's also the perfect time for competitive parents to fuel their inner fire. Standing in the tight, cramped bathroom at the family-friendly restaurant the Olive Garden, I was happy to escape the noisy and chaotic soccer team luncheon and, frankly, just relieved to be relieving myself!

My drifting thoughts snap to attention when I hear Teri, a mother from our team, on her cell phone in one of the stalls loudly discussing wins and losses with whom else? Lil, Luke's wife.

When she hangs up, she announces that the Titans (Luke and Lil's daughter's team) had lost their game at the finals. Lil assured her that their loss was because of the turf field.

Later that night, Carter's team (the Warriors) and the Titans had their team parties at the same pizza parlor. It was a long walk to the back where the teams were seated. I had already passed Luke, who barely smiled. His small eyes darted around nervously as I strolled by.

I'm just steps away from my seat when I see flashing sequins approaching me. I look down at my jeans and T-shirt to confirm that I am, indeed, dressed appropriately for the occasion and venue. I try to pick up my pace and look the other way as I greet my friend Rita.

My efforts, however, are for naught.

As I feel a hand touch my shoulder, I look up past the blinking sequins into the very concerned eyes of Lil. She softens her voice and whispers, "I'm sorry for your loss."

Truly, I am dumbfounded with confusion.

"What?" I ask. "I'm not sure what you're talking about. Nobody close to me has died recently."

Her face quickly brightens as she says with a smile, "Oh, I mean your daughter's team. They lost their game today."

I glance over at the next table and see Carter with a huge grin on her face as she throws her head back and cackles with a teammate.

"Actually, Lil, we had a great day," I say. "The girls played hard and they're having a lot of fun."

Lil walks away wordlessly in haste. Her sequins flashing like a lit up scoreboard.

S.B FRIED

My neighbor has kids that don't know how to "pretend play" when they come over. It's so sad. Their parents are so busy running them to sports and tutors, that these kids don't know how to be kids.

-J.R.

## CHAPTER 5

# Simon Says Play Basketball.
# Simon Says Play Softball.
# Simon Says Play Volleyball.
# Play Soccer!

M OST KIDS IN Swankville begin their tour de sports in January with competitive basketball, which overlaps into competitive indoor soccer, which then overlaps into competitive softball, which then overflows, into competitive swimming, which then brings us to summer. Don't get me wrong. It doesn't end there, it's just that that was a really long sentence and I figured you were getting my point.

Angela, a very sweet girl and friend of Carter's, is actually a casualty of this overscheduled sports mania that is sweeping Swankville. During a recent soccer game, she caught the ball mid-field with her hands rather than kick it with her foot. She stared down at it with round shocked eyes as if to say, "How did that happen?"

When her mother asked her just that as she trotted off the field, she replied honestly, "I thought I was playing basketball." That, in fact, was the next game she was heading off to after soccer.

One day after this happened I mentioned to the high school soccer coach how odd I thought it was that children so young were playing so many different sports at the competitive level. I didn't know if this was happening everywhere or just in Swankville.

Not at all surprised, he nodded agreeably.

"I tell parents all the time that if they want their child playing at a higher level, like so many do, then perhaps they should focus on just one or two sports as opposed to four or five, which is quickly becoming the norm," he said.

For Angela, the level of play within sports isn't her problem. Not getting time to play with her friends is.

## Simon Says Don't Play

I just finished putting the laundry away upstairs when I heard Angela, who was at our house before soccer practice, crying hysterically. Her head was bent over and her hands covered her eyes as her small shoulders shook with sobs.

I put my hand gently on her back and asked, "What's wrong? I've never seen you without a big smile on your face."

Carter quickly answered for her, "Mom, we were planning a sleepover, and Angela is sad because she plays too many sports and can't ever have sleepovers."

I know that Angela has gymnastics three afternoons a week, soccer year-around, and swim team—not to mention the occasional basketball season that triggered the momentary soccer fiasco. That being said, I relied on my psych 101 training and employed my "active listening" skills.

"So what I'm hearing you say is that you wish you had some more free time?" I ask her as I give her a soothing hug that I know always helps my kids. I take it a step further because her tears are heartbreaking and I know that nothing is probably going to change for her, at least not in the near future.

"Well, your mom made it sound like maybe you'll be cutting back on gymnastics next year and that should help free up some of your time."

She nodded, but the distress was still swimming in her eyes. In between hiccupped breaths she said, "Yeah, but if it's not my sport then it's Colby's or Tyler's sports. There's no time for sleepovers or even a play-date."

I dab away her tears with a tissue and do my best at reassuring her that something will work out.

As I head back down the stairs, I recall a day last Winter when Carter had wanted Angela to come over to play, but I reminded her that we can't ask anymore because she doesn't have any free time and it only makes her feel bad to have to say, "no."

Then, one day soon after, her mom drove past our house while we were out front and she slowed down to say "hello." Angela threw

S.B FRIED

open the door and darted out to join Carter on the tree-swing before the car barely rolled to a stop.

"Mom, can I skip gymnastics today and play at Carter's?"

Her mom hesitated for a moment and then shrugged her shoulders and said, "Sure, why not? There's a substitute in gym class anyway. Go ahead and play."

I smiled. Carter and Angela jumped up and down in excitement and enthusiasm that only young girls can generate.

Her mom said, "I feel bad. She's always asking to play with her friends, but we don't have time with all of her sports. This will be her first play-date since summertime."

It is now January. Otherwise known, in the native tongue of the Swankvillains, as basketball season.

My mom says kids should be
pushed to their max in order
to achieve something close to
perfection.

-Marlene

## CHAPTER 6

# Carter is Nimble, Carter is Quick

*Knock Her Down, Lickity Split*

I WATCH WIDE-EYED AS two of Carter's teammates knock her to the ground at basketball practice. Coincidentally, they are the daughters of very intense moms who compare their girls with Carter. I watch her get up and limp off to the sidelines crying. Within hours, our worst fears come to fruition.

Her ankle is broken.

The team's coach said Carter was one of the top four players on the team. In a matter of seconds, she went from being the one to watch to the one that would, for the rest of the season, do the watching.

She returned to the court the very next day on crutches. Not to play, of course, but to continue to support her team. She learned an early lesson about what it really means to be a true team member.

Reactions from the Swankvillain sideliners were a bit surprising.

As we approach the court, the Swankvillain inquisition starts firing on all pistons. The questions all come in twos. The first one is meant to distract while the second packs a thinly veiled punch. They go something like this:

"Oh, what happened? Is there permanent damage?"

"How long will she be out? Is this going to affect her skill level?"

"Do you think she'll be back this season? Are you going to get your money back?"

"You're not seriously planning on attending all the games even though she can't play, are you? Is this the end of her basketball career?"

The coach's next words speak volumes and are more appropriate than any answer I can muster at this point.

"Carter will not be the only injury this year," he says. "In fact, most of you will have an injury at some point. Carter is the ideal player as she showed up in full uniform to support her team even though she is out for two months. Thank you, Carter, for being a true team player and showing us what this game is all about."

Two days later, I'm walking back home with Carter after watching another practice courtside. I'm pulling seventy pounds worth of Carter and Jake in a wagon with one hand, gripping the dog leash with the other hand, and strategically using both arms to wipe the dripping sweat from my eyes. Of course, this is the perfect time for a comment from the peanut gallery, but no one is around . . . oh wait, yes there is.

"You are soooo funny," the familiar shrill of Lil's voice vibrates against my eardrums.

I look up to see her pedaling rapidly on a big red-and-white bike toward the gym.

Exasperated, I take the bait.

"What do you mean?" I ask her.

"Carter can't even play, and you take her to all the practices and games anyway," she says giggling.

I know I should be offended, but for some reason, all I can think about is that man-child Pee-wee Herman, riding around on his red-and-white bike, dispensing irrelevant nonsequiturs like "I know you are, but what am I?" Hmmm, interesting.

Growing up in this town, most mothers strive for perfection in their children, mine being one of the worst I've ever seen.

-John

# CHAPTER 7

# The Tortoise and the Hare

*I'm Forty, but You're a Shorty, Na, Na, Na-Na, Na!*

FIELD DAY AT Rebecca and Carter's school is an exciting way to end the school year. The entire campus is full of glee as kids partake in a myriad of organized games and activities that have little to do with winning and losing and everything to do with pure fun.

When I arrive, I immediately scan the crowd for my girls.

Suddenly, I spot Lil. She is the only adult participating in the relay race against, whom else, my nine-year-old daughter.

I stare in disbelief as Carter darts ahead of Lil. Attempting to catch up with Carter before she crosses the finish line, I hear Lil yell, "You aren't going to beat me, Carter!"

"Oh, Lil, you are soooo funny."

I'm a babysitter for a family with three kids and I have to pick them up from school and drop them off at all of their activities early. Their mom always reminds me to drop them off early so they get noticed.

-Alicia

## CHAPTER 8

# I'm late I'm Late, for a Very Important Date!!!

"REBECCA DID THEY move ice skating team try out practices to three-thirty? I have been taking you at four!" I ask in a panic.

"They didn't move them. It's just that all of the parents want their kids to make it so badly that they bring them a half hour earlier than the actual time it starts."

"Of course they do," I grumble under my breath. Once again parents find new ways of upping the ante. Now, it looks like my kid is late by a half hour to something that she is really exactly on time for.

Come to think of it, this has been happening at other practices lately, too.

Aha! I'll just turn my clocks back an hour a couple of months before daylight savings begins. That ought to give me a leg up on the Swankvillains—not to mention the rest of the population west of the Colorado Rockies!

I knew a guy whose parents would make him play through all his injuries. They never took the doctor's advice to rest the injury and the guy ended up with such a bad knee that he couldn't even play in college.

-Jim

## CHAPTER 9

# Sticks and Stones May Break My Bones but Cheerleading is Going to Kill Me!!

"MOM, MY ANKLE really hurts," Rebecca cries, as she hobbles into the car.

My gut tells me she must have broken a bone because my girls are tough cookies and the only time either of them cries from an injury is when they have fractured or sprained something. Like their mother, hurt feelings seem to move them to tears quicker than a bump or a bruise.

I drive her straight to the ER.

"Well, she's definitely broken her ankle," the doctor says matter-of-factly. "I'll need to cast it and then examine it again in a couple of weeks."

He sees my concern, and rather than allay my fears, he issues this warning, "I've seen more concussions and broken bones from cheerleading than any other sport, including football."

Back in the car, I recite in my mind all the famous lines from that one-woman show we all get cast in the day our children are born. You know, "The Mother's Monologue."

*Why did I let her try-out? She has to quit. It's too dangerous. But she really loves it and wants to participate. How can I tell her she can't be a part of the team after she tried out and made it. Maybe just this year and that's it. I wonder if they make special cheerleading helmets . . ."*

"What happened to 'Dribble it, Pass it, Let's Make a Basket?'" I ask Becca. She just stares at me like I'm speaking a foreign language.

Clearly, middle-school cheerleading has drastically changed over the last twenty-five years. Let me break it down for you:

- 8-person squads are now 20-member teams.
- Football and Basketball games have been replaced by competitions.
- Pro-life pyramids have been remodeled into death defying formations that shoot out herkys, pikes, and toe-touches, like bullets out of a Nerf gun.

- 1-minute chants have evolved into 12-minute cheer and dance extravaganzas worthy of a gold medal (or for you dance moms out there, a high-high gold-plated silver, with a lemon twist and a cherry on top!)

My point is cheerleading is no longer just a fun extra-curricular activity. It is an athletic sport that demands gymnastic classes, dance training, and Swankville's secret weapon—private instruction.

The Upside: Top universities across the country now award cheerleading scholarships. *Rah-Rah-Sis-Boom-Bah!*

The Downside: Your college student might be spending his or her first semester in a full-body cast. *Gimme an "O", Gimme a "U", Gimme a "C", Gimme an "H." What does it spell?*

I work at a local dance/costume store and see little girls with their crazy stage moms all the time. A mom actually made me cry at work because I wasn't fast enough when I was waiting on her. The moms overwork their little divas to achieve something they never could.

-Gail

## CHAPTER 10

# All the Pretty Maids in a Row

*But Mine is the Prettiest*

WHEN DOES COMPETITIVE parenting really begin? Is there an actual moment when we enter the ring with gloves raised, hear the announcer inside our heads say, "Let's get ready to ruuummmble," and then listen for the bell to go ding-ding—or, in my case, wait for the parade of ding-a-lings?

Without even realizing it, the competitive bug crawls up on us from the moment our children are born. It's as though we push them out during labor and then just keep right on pushing.

Mom #1: "How much does she weigh?"
Mom #2: "Eight pounds, eight ounces. How about your daughter?"
Mom #1: "Oh, she's only seven pounds, four ounces, but very long. The doctor says she's going to be tall and skinny—like a ballerina."
Mom #2: "Well, the size of my baby's head is above average. She's already in the seventy-fifth percentile."
Mom #1: "My gosh! She's got a huge head!"
Mom #2: "You know what they say, 'big head, big brain.'"
Mom #1: "Well then, she's bound to be a little genius."

And so it begins.

I stepped into the ring when my oldest daughter Rebecca was five, and we joined the recreational activity circuit. This is also the same time I met and became friends with Karen and Fretful Fran. We all have daughters the same age. Karen has Jennifer and Sophia while Fran has Reagan and Penelope.

"Hi, Sasha, it's Fran. I need you to call me back. I'm planning Reagan's fall schedule, and I want to make sure our girls are in the same classes. I can't wait much longer, or they'll fill up, so call me as soon as you can. I've left you several messages, but haven't heard back, so call me. Call me at home, or try me on my cell—just call."

I'm listening to this message on my way to work, and I can literally feel the car closing in on me. It's as though the oversized SUV I'm driving has just shrunk down to a two-door Mini-Cooper that has suddenly become boxed in by four large semi trucks.

Once the claustrophobia passes, I call Fran back and coordinate dance class with her.

Becca loves to dance, and I love watching her. One of the highlights of dance lessons at this age is during Halloween when the girls all come dressed up in their costumes. Practically from the first class in early September, the girls start talking about what they want to be.

In true Becca style, she decided nearly a year in advance that she wanted to be a fairy. We bought her a pretty lavender fairy costume over the summer since she rarely, if ever, changes her mind.

While she chats enthusiastically about her fairy costume, Fran's daughter Reagan speaks excitedly about her own plans to be Batman.

"Bat *girl*," Fran corrects her daughter.

"She can borrow Becca's black coat and mask that she wore for her recital last summer," I offer. "It's very girlie and just adorable! It could be a good start for a Batgirl costume."

"No thanks, it won't be necessary," she replies. "She's actually not going to be Batman or Batgirl at all for Halloween."

The infamous class finally arrives, and I watch with such joy as Becca jumps and spins in her costume that she's waited months to wear. I love watching her look at herself in the mirror in awe of her wings flapping about.

My euphoria is sharply interrupted by Fran's squeaky voice.

"We're late, Reagan, and you need to catch up with your class," Fran demands. "Please hurry up, and don't forget your wand."

I look up to see Reagan flutter through the door in the most gorgeous fairy costume I've ever seen. Between the multilayers of tulle, the ornate wings, and the illuminating sparkles, even I start to believe that these delicate winged nymphs might be for real.

After class, Becca skips up to me and says, "Reagan is a fairy too." Her voice drops to a whisper. "She didn't want to be a fairy. She wanted to be Batman."

I simply smile and nod in agreement. *Holy crazy dance mom, Batman!*

## Round Two (Ding-a-ling)— Fretful Fran versus Simmering Sasha

All was calm and pleasant at the dance studio as several of us watched the teacher place our daughters in their designated positions for their tap number, "Ringling Bros.," for the upcoming recital.

All of a sudden, Fran sidles up next to us at the observation window, pressing her face and hands against the glass in order to get a better view. Her high-pitched squeal about how cute they all look triggers an involuntary twitch in my left eye. I immediately begin my deep-breathing exercises, but soon discover I'm wasting perfectly good oxygen.

Fran discretely moves closer to me and whispers, "I hope they don't intend on putting Sophia next to my precious Penelope because Sophia doesn't dance very well, and she'll cause Penelope to mess up."

I cringe at Fran's relentless obsession about where her daughter may or may not be placed.

"Do you think Karen will mind if I say something?"

She's totally serious, and I'm totally disgusted by what she has just said. I let the wave of nausea pass through me before I respond.

"Yes, Fran, Karen will mind, and her feelings will be very hurt if she thinks you believe her two-year-old daughter will mess

Penelope up during the recital," I say. "I'm sure all the girls will do just fine no matter who they are standing next to."

We turn our attention back to the moms who are now discussing what circus animal their daughters are choosing to be for the show.

We've got one elephant with an unusually short trunk, a cute billowy sheep, a darling brown monkey, and not surprisingly, a gaggle of cute kitty-like tigers.

When someone asks a suspiciously quiet Fran what animal Penelope will be representing, she replies, "I'm not telling because I don't want anyone else to come in the same costume."

*Two hours later.*

I'm at home cooking dinner when the telephone rings. It's Karen calling to tell me that not only did Fran say something to her about not wanting their girls next to each other, but she also told the teachers to be sure and move Penelope.

My response?

Let's just say that the broccoli wasn't the only thing steaming in my kitchen!

*Twenty-four hours later.*

I'm standing with my darling tiger and her other furry friends, waiting until it is their turn to perform. Penelope is the last to arrive. She toddles up to the group in a black leotard, diamond tiara, and a bright red boa with feathers flying everywhere.

"What circus animal are you supposed to be," asks the monkey.

"A ladybug," replies Penelope as she takes her new position out on the stage.

Throughout the dance, there are the usual oohs and aahhs, until suddenly the entire audience lurches forward in their seats and gasps.

Penelope, the little red-and-black ladybug—you know, the kind you see doing tricks at the circus—took a few missteps and tripped over her flowing boa. She recovered, and I must say, was a pretty cute ladybug. Her mother, however, was a lady bugged.

## Round Three—Type A Tabitha Goes Coo-Coo Over a Tutu

In theory, dance recitals exist to showcase the culmination of the dancers' hard work and to justify the hard-earned dollars that pour out of their parents' pockets throughout the season. Mothers and fathers, mostly mothers, relish this moment and don't want to miss a second of their future prima ballerina's stunning performance. The pin that pops a small leak into this boastful balloon, however, is the knowledge that one or two mothers will have to give up their seat in the audience and volunteer to be the backstage mom to take care of bathroom breaks and other potential catastrophes.

I volunteered this year to corral the "circus animals" for a couple of reasons. First, my daughter wants me backstage with her, and second, I don't feel slighted in the least because I've been attentively watching her all year long in her classes and know the routine by heart. I do not volunteer for this position as a martyr; I genuinely don't mind it, and I know the other moms are very appreciative—well, most of them.

"Excuse me? Are you Sasha? I was told you are the backstage mom that is responsible for some of the girls," Type A Tabitha asked accusingly when she came to retrieve her daughter.

Sheathing my claws, I calmly smiled and nodded my head.

"Well, Adriana's tutu must have ripped on your watch. I checked her from head to toe before I took my seat in the audience, and I know she was flawless for her performance," said the tiger mom. I mean one of the *tiger's* moms. "It ruined her entire performance for me. I invited friends and family to watch her, and I'm so embarrassed that she had a rip in her tutu."

"Let's see, there are fifteen girls in my group," I began. "I did a lipstick check and a bathroom run, but in the several times I've volunteered to do this, I've never had issues with the tutus."

As she stared at me wide-eyed, I used the time to gather my defenses and asked, "Which girl is your daughter?" She pointed her out of the crowd that I had indeed been chaperoning.

"She did have to use the restroom," I offered. "Perhaps it happened when she was coming out of the stall."

"Humph!" snorted Tabitha. "I can't believe you allowed her to rip it!"

I can't believe I'm allowing her to rip into me!

Type A Tabitha's anger and embarrassment over her daughter's flawed costume completely overshadowed the two-and-a-half minutes that she could have been enjoying her little girl joyfully dancing about on the stage. Is this the reflection her daughter should see when she looks into her mother's eyes?

If it is, then that is truly too, too bad.

You get pressured to be the best at your sport, instead of just playing it for the fun of it. This is what killed baseball for me. I used to love to play it, but the pressure from my dad to be the best ever just turned me off of the sport completely.

—Craig

## CHAPTER 11

# Eanie, Meanie, Miney, Moe
# Kids Played Eight Games in a Row
# Though They Hollered
# They Couldn't Go
# 'Til Their Parents Came to Blows!

"GO, LEELEE!" OUR pitcher's mom cheers loudly as her daughter throws her tenth strike this inning alone. At least this time she's cheering on her own kid rather than yelling disrespectfully at the umpire. I eye her cautiously from behind the bleachers where I'm watching Jake play. My Swankvillain-radar is on high alert, and warning flares are going up all around me.

It is late afternoon on Sunday, and our whole family of five is enduring the sweltering summer heat while watching the eighth game of Carter's traveling softball tournament. She played four games on Saturday and has already played three games today. Oh yeah, and she, like all the girls on her team and the team she's playing, is nine years old. So in case you think you read this wrong or added up these numbers incorrectly, let me assure you that you have *not*.

*12 nine-year-old girls × 8 softball games – 2 days ÷ 90-degree heat + 24 aggressively competitive parents = criminal behavior.*

No lie. No matter how you do the math, it still adds up to child abuse!

So here I am a couple of innings into the championship game with both the temperature and the tempers running high. Leah's spirited mom starts in again. "Come on, you've got this, LeeLee. It's your game!" she shouts. "You are doing this alone!"

My head snaps around quicker than LeeLee's fast pitch. Did she just credit her own daughter for our team winning this game so far? Only a Swankvillain! Annoyed, but not entirely shocked, I settle on the bleachers to watch a softball game that is about to reach a fever pitch.

**Strike one:** One of the dads from the other team is sitting on the bench below me, and he is huge! I mean, steroid huge, with muscles and veins popping out all over his body. He watches intently as his daughter comes up to bat. I'm sure she's not on steroids, but I have to admit, when she swings a bat, fond memories of the bionic woman come to mind. The ball is pitched, cracks against the bat, and smacks right into the nose of one of our own players. Blood sprays everywhere as some of the girls start crying. Even Carter reaches the end of her rope and sits on the bleachers with her dad. Before things can even settle down from the bloody nose, however, another curve ball is thrown.

**Strike two:** Just as the opponent hit the ball, our catcher caught it, and the runner on third, who stands over five feet tall and weighs 115 pounds, runs for the play; but instead of sliding into home plate she puts her hands out and shoves our catcher to the ground to avoid the out. It was intentionally aggressive, and instead of being appalled, their coaches and parents erupt into cheers. When the ump sides with them and calls the play safe, the parents turn nasty. Leah's mom immediately yells out so everyone can hear, "That's not fair that they have such fat players who can knock down our small, petite girls." Her use of the f-word leaves me speechless. There is no greater sin in my playbook than for a mother to call young girls *fat*. Meanwhile, the catcher's mom runs to home plate to help her hysterical and injured daughter. Then another mom turns her ire toward the ump and screams, "I have watched hundreds of softball games between all three of my girls at the high school level, recreational level, and competitive level, and I have never witnessed such poor behavior or unfair calls by an umpire." Swankville is now in full swing.

**Strike three:** My eyes dart down the sideline just in time to see two of our dads gang up on the muscle man and his barbell buddies. A full brawl breaks out with punches thrown on both sides. Fathers are hitting each other, mothers are screaming at the top of their lungs, and sadly, twenty-two frightened young girls are crying hysterically while begging their parents to stop fighting. Stepping up to the plate, the ump finally makes the smartest call he's made all weekend, "That's it! Game over! I'm calling the game and the police if this doesn't stop immediately."

Three strikes and we're *all* out.

At my little brother's baseball game, I watched one of the player's father's break the nose of his own son's coach because he was mad that he didn't play his son enough. It was disgusting. One dad ended up in the hospital, and the other was arrested and sent to jail.

-Scott

## CHAPTER 12

# Hickory Dickory Dock
# My Dad's Gonna Clean Your Clock
# He's Big as a Moose
# from Hitting the Juice
# Why Don't You Just Take a Walk?

*D*ADDY CAME TO *sit by me in the dugout and asked me to hand him my bat. I didn't need to ask him why he needed it because I could tell the reason. We sat closely together while he held tightly onto my bat as the steroid guy and our warrior screamed at each other. I had nightmares for nights after. Why can't this town just be normal?*

Two months after the softball brawl, Carter hands me an essay she wrote for school and asks me to check it for grammar errors before turning it in the next day.

The title at the top of the page reads:

*My 5 Most Memorable Moments of This Past Summer.*

Right after fireworks on 4th of July and bringing home a new puppy, is a very well written account of what took place during that infamous softball game through the eyes of an impressionable nine-year-old child. If ever, any of us thought for even a moment that our actions and words did not impact our own children and their peers, then it's time we think again. Her recollection of the story was quite eye opening.

*"Yo! Man, what's your problem. That's my daughter you're talking smack about," said our enemy.*

*Of course our enemy happened to be 6' 3" and 300 pounds of full muscle. Some say all he did was go to the gym, while others stuck to the most logical reason of all—steroids. He stood up to his tallest and sneered at the man who was apparently talking smack about his giant of a daughter. Our team's warrior stood to his tallest at 5'9" about a foot separating the two. Not to mention our warrior had a jiggly stomach.*

Our warrior answered, "I ain't talking smack about anybody, but your huge daughter (he used a word that I cannot write) can't run into our catcher and send her flying like she did."

"Well, I'm about to make you run crying if you ain't dead that is," said our enemy.

"Bring it on!" our warrior said, which is the dumbest thing he could have said in my opinion.

Just as our enemy was about to kill our warrior with his fists (which were both the size of small watermelons), the umpires and other parents broke it up saying they were about to call the police.

My dad held my baseball bat for protection. Luckily they separated us and we were pulled out of the next tournament because they would be there. I think you can tell that the game had ended. Sadly, we lost because they were in the lead at the moment the ump called the game.

I still have nightmares and questions to this day. Why couldn't this just be a normal town? Then again there wouldn't be any excitement if everyone was normal. That's what makes us, us.

Yes, unfortunately, it is. Welcome to Suburbia, USA.

Kids will not know how to take care of themselves when mommy and daddy aren't there to fix their problems. They will struggle to become independent and lead lives for themselves.

-Brian

## CHAPTER 13

# My, What a Dreadful Big Mouth You Have!

*All the Better to Bite Your Head Off, Dearie!*

I'M NAUSEATED AND tired. In other words, I'm in my first trimester, pregnant with my third child. Although running the Girl Scout cookie booth outside of the local grocery store with my daughter's troop to sell Girl Scout cookies isn't at the top of my list, nothing makes me feel better than seeing my child happy. This is why I'm a troop leader. I want my girls to have this experience as I remember fondly selling cookies and singing at convalescent homes, knowing that I was making the world a better place by these small deeds.

As Carter *do-si-dos* proudly and enthusiastically up to each potential customer and charming them all with her bright smile, I *tag along* behind her, basking in her exuberance while trying to remind myself that I'm not rocking back and forth on an aluminum boat in the middle of the Pacific Ocean.

Just as we're finding our groove, I spot my neighbor Nelly and her daughter Polly across the parking lot set up in front of the drug store. They look up and make a bee-line right toward us.

Nelly, in the lead and fiercely swinging her arms, shouts out in our direction "Oh, we have a little *COM-PE-TI-TION*." Polly, with her head lowered, trails behind her mother.

"Well, it's one thing to have booths set up so close to one another, but I do hope you won't be selling cookies to anyone on our street. Please stay on your own street," demands Nelly. "Have you been to the Solomons, the Saddlers, or the Stevensons?"

I feel my eyes dilate and my nose flare in search of more oxygen as my body prepares itself for a fight-or-flight situation. With patience that's wearing *thinner than the mint cookies* my daughter is selling, I calmly assure Nelly that Carter sold just one box to her next-door neighbor, but requested that he not buy more than that as Polly would most likely be coming by to sell to him as well. After all, the Girl Scout way *is* about sharing, *isn't* it?

"Good!" is all Nelly could muster before stalking off.

*Gee*, I think to myself. At the very least, she could have said, "*Thank U Berry Munch!*"

## John Jacob Jingleheimer Schmidt— Have You Ever Tried to Spell That?

I just trailed loving kisses on my daughter's face and told her good-bye as she was venturing off for school. I take a moment to enjoy the warm fall morning, breathe deeply, and gather my thoughts on how to best use the free time that lay before me. Suddenly, Elaine and her husband sidle up next to me.

"You know you ruined the cookie booth for Mollie and Dollie last night," accuses Elaine.

Her husband and spousal ally harshly adds, "Yeah, they were really upset that you spelled their names wrong on their cookie bags. Not to mention the fact that you have no idea which one is which."

"At the very least, it'd be nice if you could take the time to find out the correct spelling of their names," says Elaine.

Stunned and hurt, I can feel my defensive shackles beginning to rise. *I know how to spell CRRAAAAZZYY*, I think to myself.

Instead, I say aloud, "Well, I'm kind of busy volunteering to lead two Brownie troops."

By the time I get home, my defensiveness is replaced by guilt for my curt reply, so I decide to send an e-mail formally apologizing for not taking the time to look up the proper spelling of her daughters' names in the directory. I assure her that I will be more careful in the future. I also add that I too have a different name that is always being misspelled or mispronounced, but am not sensitive to it because my mom taught me early on that it would just build character. To this day, even as an adult, my name continues to be slaughtered, but I just laugh it off and realize how right my mother was!

Two days go by, and no response from Elaine.

I decide to call her.

She answers the phone and says, "Sasha, I have *twins!* I am really busy . . ."

*Click!*

Oh no, she didn't!

Yes, by golly, she did. She actually hung up on me. I felt like I had been kicked in the stomach. I really liked Elaine and appreciated that she supported me as the troop leader when I took over after the former leader had to step down early. I feel hurt and sad for a second time.

What I never got a chance to explain to Elaine was that during the time selling cookies at the cookie booth, her daughters' didn't mention at all to me their misspelled name. I thought they were crying because people weren't buying cookies from us. So I kept them company at the expense of hanging out with my own two daughters.

You would expect that I would have a story about how the children were behaving badly at a Girl Scout event by being mean or catty to one another.

Nope!

All the girls did just fine. If there were any mishaps, no doubt they would be age appropriate. After all, they're children. Instead, I once again come away with a disappointing parental moment. I guess children really are fine—until we, in the name of parenting, screw them up!

## Girl Scout Way—Turn Right? . . . *Wrong!*

"Do you think we can just put Sasha's name down as the leader, but we can really run the troop?" the e-mail read.

This was clearly not meant for my eyes, but it was inadvertently sent to me when a handful of moms were strategizing a way to control everything without becoming formally responsible for anything. I actually read it several times in utter disbelief.

Let me get this straight. This mom who enrolled her daughter in Girl Scouts to teach her about honesty, leadership, and integrity, in less than twenty words, encouraged *lying* about a *leadership* role in an organization designed to promote—what's the word? Oh yeah, *integrity*!

The best or better life isn't always the one that makes you a better person.

−Janelle

# CHAPTER 14

# I'll Huff and Puff and Blow Your House Down

*Because It Looks Better Than Mine!*

THE SUN IS shining brightly on this early morning, and I'm feeling quite good as I jog through the park. A man I recognize from my neighborhood starts heading over to me.

When I wave my greeting, he stops me in my tracks.

"So you are the one I have to thank for my wife's recent interest in meeting with contractors. She told me, 'We have to do something to our house now, or we won't have the biggest, most amazing house in the neighborhood.'"

Whenever you take on a large home renovation, everyone is in your business, if not your home. One morning, I actually woke up to a woman and some of her friends touring my downstairs foundation that was just a shell at the time. I couldn't recall posting a sign that read: "Welcome Swankvillains. Please tour even while we sleep."

Since Jim's wife is Nelly, the one who lectured me about who to sell Girl Scout cookies to, I am not at all surprised by what her husband is admitting. Their beautiful, New England cottage-style home looks as though it's been cut directly out of a glossy magazine and placed in our neighborhood. The white garden boxes under the shuttered windows always have bright pink flowers cascading down to complete the perfect picture.

Well, if Nelly is inspired by our home remodel or by a more primal urge she has referred to as *COM-PE-TI-TION*, I'll never know. While I'm not immune to the Swankville syndrome of one-upping the Jones's (that would be "keeping up's" ugly cousin), I can say that our decision to remodel was as much about function as it was form.

I became pregnant with our third child at the same time we decided to stay in Swankville and give up our dream home and a less-complicated lifestyle in Montana. I was homesick before we even moved, and I wasn't the only one suffering. My mom would come to my daughters' dance classes, wearing her dark sunglasses to hide her tears. She didn't want us to leave, and I realized being close to family was what was most important.

Two months into the reconstruction, I miscarried. What began as an exciting project quickly turned into a grueling process. My contractor called me relentlessly on my cell phone saying, "Sasha, I need you to go to Home Depot right now and make a decision on the flooring." I found absolutely no joy in any of the construction at this point.

People commented to me all the time that I was so lucky to design my new home and how exciting it must be to own the biggest house in the neighborhood. Emotionally drained, I looked at them flatly and said, "I'd rather have my baby."

One day following my miscarriage, a mom from my daughter's preschool approached me and said, "Sorry about your miscarriage, but at least you have your house."

"Mmm-hmm," I replied, knowing that it didn't matter what the outside of a home looked like. It's the inside that counts. I turned and walked away, feeling sick to my empty stomach.

I lived in Arkansas growing up. There it was all about being popular. My mom was constantly on me about being friends with the right crowd and making cheerleading. I ended up dropping out of school, moving to California, and having a baby at seventeen.

—Jemma

# CHAPTER 15

# Ring around Rosie

*Crassness, Brashness, We All Fall Down*

DICTIONARIES LOOSELY DEFINE the new millennium phenomenon *playgroup* as a small group of moms who get together on a regular basis in order to provide early socialization opportunities for their non-school-aged children (usually between the ages of three and five).

If Swankville published its own dictionary, I imagine the definition might read something like this:

**playgroup (play-group)** (1) a kiddie cult for budding geniuses and their mothers who come together to compare, critique, and compete;
(2) gathering of moms in their thirties and forties with junior high angst; (3) the best of times and the worst of times.

No matter the definition, the fact is, I was a proud playgroupie. I bought into it hook, line, and Binky.

I liked Rosie, the cult leader, right away when I introduced myself to her over the phone and inquired about joining her playgroup. We spoke for twenty minutes and seemed to have a lot in common. I could hardly wait to meet her and was even more excited to finally have a playgroup for my first baby Rebecca, who was just six months old. Before hanging up, we planned to meet at my house two days later. Our first time would be just the two of us so we could really get to know each other.

When she knocked on my door a couple of days later, I opened it with anxious anticipation. To my surprise, her face didn't match her engaging voice. Instead of a small woman with dark hair, I greeted a lady with blond hair that hung limply down her back and whose bright white teeth made her look younger than her thirty years. Her five-foot-eleven-inch stature foreshadowed her large presence.

"Wow, you're so skinny. You must have already lost your baby weight," she says before even stepping over the threshold. This would be the first of many times she comments on my weight over the next five years.

After getting together alone a few more times, Rosie finally brings me into the fold. I am the newcomer to this existing group of six women, all of whom were coworkers. There is not much effort to discuss anything besides their work stories, but I'm just genuinely happy to be included.

The other playgroupies include Leila, Jamie, Amelia (Rosie's favorite), and Annabelle, the friend I remain closest with even today.

I hardly missed a meeting, convinced that my six-month-old would be better off because of these weekly get-togethers. During the first few years, I felt happy, so surely my baby was happy as well. When you put an odd number of women together for any length of time, however, drama is sure to follow. I knew red flags were popping up almost right from the beginning, but I failed to notice them because my head was down changing dirty diapers most of the time. I finally paid attention around the third year.

*Red flag 1—The Holiday Gift Exchange*: Rosie always organized the gift exchange by having each of us anonymously draw names. This year, however, she rigged the draw so that Annabelle and I would be exchanging gifts with each other. She inadvertently admitted this without ever realizing it. Now, this would not appear, on the outset, that it should be a big deal, but Rosie felt threatened by the friendship Anabelle and I shared, so this was her way of remaining in control of the group and her relationships. *This was the whisper telling me, "It's time to wrap it up."*

*Red flag 2—The Birthday Party*: When I sent birthday invitations out for Becca's fourth birthday party at the ice skating rink, Rosie told all the playgroupies not to RSVP or attend because it would be too dangerous. Her real issue was that I randomly asked a few of the guests to donate a book in Becca's name in lieu of a gift in an attempt to teach my child the value in giving to others. While my intentions were honorable, I understand that this was not the best venue for teaching a life lesson and that modeling proper behavior as a parent is much more effective.

Nobody from the playgroup attended the party, and needless to say, my feelings were hurt. When Becca opened her last gift and pulled out a rag doll dressed in a brown-and-purple plaid dress with yellow-and-orange skinny stripes running through it, my reaction was, "Who hates us?" I had just seen this doll on clearance at the resale shop downtown. "Hey, Becca, who is that from?" I inquired. "Rosie and Riley," she said. I felt a knife in my heart. After years of giving beautiful gifts, I guess Rosie was sending a new message. When I bumped into her, I mentioned that I had seen the doll downtown. She hesitated, then said that her husband had picked up the wrong gift and that he insists on bringing over another one. *This was the tap on my shoulder telling me, "Hey, playgroupie, you're skating on thin ice."*

**Red flag 3**—*The Breast Pump*: I handed over my three-hundred-dollar breast pump to Rosie, knowing in my gut that it was not the right thing to do. I always thought of it as a booby-trap, and, ironically, that's what it turned out to be.

First of all, I knew I wanted another child; and no matter how you cut it, this is just not sanitary. Second, I knew she could afford one herself. However, I sensed that I was being pushed out of the playcult and felt an irrational need to please the leader. She had finally gotten pregnant with her desired baby boy after years of spinning sperm, and she evidently caught me at a weak moment.

During the months she was using it, I endured her increasingly cold shoulder at the playcult meetings. But after receiving a message on my answering machine about how she had just spent over three hundred dollars at the local swanky baby boutique, I was fed up!

One day on my way to the gym, I knocked on her door and asked for my breast pump back.

Four years later, when I had my third baby, I pulled out the pump. Although I still got it to work, I noticed that she had stuck a screw in it to hold a loose part of it together. *This was the slap in my face telling me, "Sasha, you've been screwed." I take a deep breath and remember something I should have listened to long ago, and that is a quote from Buddha: "Sometimes it is better to walk alone than to follow the path of fools."*

*Today, Buddha might have revised it a bit: "Sometimes it is better to walk alone than to follow the path of boobs."*

My mom always seemed to be under pressure and stressed out. I think it caused her to push my brothers and sisters and me too hard. She not only expected a lot from us and herself, but from everyone around her too.

-Amanda

## CHAPTER 16

# Bibbity Bobbity Poo

*A Tail of Two Female Dogs*

I ROUND THE CORNER armed with all the essentials of a well-burdened mom out for a walk on a rainy afternoon. I've got my two kids, my neighbor's two kids, a baby stroller, a large umbrella, and our dog—Bibbity.

One of the kids is holding Bibbity's leash when the literal poop hits the figurative fan. Unaware of the calamity that apparently took place in a nearby bush, I am justifiably confused when a woman rolls down her window and yells, "Aren't you going to pick that up?"

"What do you mean?" I ask honestly since she could be referring to a number of items I'm precariously balancing in my arms.

She asks more specifically, "Are you going to pick up your dog's poop?"

I look around, trying to locate the offending evidence while calmly explaining that I'm always conscientious about cleaning up after my dog, but my hands are full, and I can't even see it!

My dog may have been done taking her dump, but this woman was clearly not done dumping on me.

"It's people like you that are ruining our parks by not cleaning up after their dogs," she scolds.

One of the kids points to the bush where the dog has taken care of her business. "Oh," I say, trying to maintain my composure in front of four impressionable children. "Well, fortunately, this is not a park or anyone's yard for that matter. It's an alleyway with dirt and bushes, and she pooped off the path."

Just then, the hostile woman's kids climb wordlessly into her minivan with their heads lowered. Obviously, this is not the first time they've seen their mother in a crappy mood. As if she has not already set a good-enough example in front of everyone's children about the importance of keeping the community clean, her last parting shot proves that she does not hold herself to the same standard. Pulling slowly away from the curb, she rolls down her window one last time and yells out, "You *bitch!*"

Even Bibbity knew she was talking to me.

## Bibbity Bobbity Poo—Number Two

Although my initial anger over that stinky situation took a few days to subside, I did finally come to terms with the fact that this woman must have really been having a bad day. I was merely a victim of a random act of violence—Swankville's version of a drive-by shouting. Well, apparently in Swankville, lightning can strike twice.

My two-year-old Jake and I roll into to the park with Bibbity in tow, ready to enjoy a relaxing morning in the sun. When Jake anxiously pops out of his stroller to head to the sandbox, I realize from how large his bottom has grown that he has a very full diaper—this should have been my first sign. I secure the dog's leash under the stroller's wheel, playfully tackle Jake to the ground, and prepare for what is sure to be a very dirty job. I'm on my tenth wipe with sweat beading on my upper lip when a shadow falls across our bodies.

"Go clean up your dog's mess, now," a woman's voice booms above my head.

I look up startled, thinking to myself, *You've got to be kidding me. I know Swankville is a wealthy town, but are there really extra funds for a dog-crap task force?*

I respond quietly, but firmly, "As soon as I'm done here, I will."

Gathering up my diaper-changing supplies, I keep an eye on my son as he toddles toward a three-year-old who is visiting the park with his dad.

The short, stout, bulldog of a woman, who I have now privately nicknamed Jaba-the-Hut, moves closer to me and points thirty feet in the distance. "It's over there. Go clean it up."

The dad of the three-year-old hears my marching orders and says sympathetically, "I'll keep my eye on him."

I take just three steps when my mother's instinctual gut kicks into high gear. No way am I going to let some stranger watch my kid just because some bully is telling me to go pick up dog poop that is not disturbing anyone at the moment.

I turn toward Jaba and say, "I will get to the poop, as I always do, as soon as I can. My son is my priority right now."

She leans heavily on the park bench with her arms crossed over her chest and stares at me with pursed lips. Her six-year-old is running around like a wild animal, disrupting other kids, but her eyes never leave me.

I walk over and sit by the dad and our two kids who are playing in the sandbox.

"She's not done with me yet," I mutter under my breath.

"She's just getting started," he agrees.

After the dad and his son bid us good-bye, Jake and I continue to play under her watchful eye. When Jake gets bored twenty minutes later, Bibbity and I follow him to the adjoining playground.

Stalking closely behind us, she says, "So you're not going to pick it up are you?"

I keep my mouth shut and ignore her for a full ten minutes. I can't believe that she would rather spend her time monitoring my behavior instead of playing with her own child.

When I finally decide it's time to leave the park, I gather up Jake, the dog, and the stroller. I pull out a plastic bag and head over to where I believe the dog poop is hiding. Making a game of it, I'm asking Jake, "Where's the pooh-pooh? Where's the pooh-pooh?" For the life of me, I can't find it anywhere!

"Over there," she yells at me. I continue my search with her hanging over my shoulder and hurling disjointed insults like, "Look at the way you dress your son."

Fed up, I turn to her and say, "You are harassing me. Please stop."

When she realizes she's not getting anywhere with me, she looks at Jake and says, "Your mommy is so messy. She's a slob."

Jake just stares up at her with his big blue eyes, points his tiny finger at her, and says, what sounds to *me*, "There's the pooh-pooh."

The woman outside the dance studio pushing her daughter to do math three grades above her grade in between dance classes could have been my mom. As a result, I have fought bulimia most of my life.

-Sara

## CHAPTER 17

# One, Two, She's Smarter Than You

*Three, Four, Just Check Her Score*

I GOT TO CARTER'S school early today and am waiting outside her classroom door for the bell to ring.

The door flies open wide, and a flood of kids run off to grab their backpacks.

Kit, the math center helper in Carter's third-grade class, trails behind them. After she and I exchange hellos, she asks me, "Can you believe our state test results? The second graders did very well, and Amanda got a perfect score," she says, referring to a student who has been in the same class with Carter since first grade.

I smile politely and listen intently to that intuitive voice inside my head, saying, *Why is she telling me about her score? Amanda isn't even her daughter. I'm Carter's mom, and her progress is all I care about. Even worse, she says it in front of Carter and two other classmates.*

"Well, I'm just thrilled with Carter's score," I reply.

## Five, Six, It's Making Carter Sick
## Seven, Eight, Though I Tell Her She's Great

During the next four weeks, Carter comes home and is constantly comparing her work to Amanda's work.

When I tell her I'm proud of her for only missing two out of twenty on her math test, she immediately reports that Amanda got a perfect score.

"Carter, you don't have to *be* the best. You just have to *do* your best," I remind her.

For the first time ever, Carter's love of school begins to wane.

"I want to switch classes," says Carter. "I'm tired of being with all the 'smarties.'"

When I inquire with the principal about moving Carter because she doesn't want to go to school anymore, she informs me that all the rooms are at full capacity, and that at this point, it's not an option.

I give the disappointing news to Carter. I try to offer comfort by telling her that, like her challenging math problems, we will try to figure it out together.

She's not humored by my analogy.

## Nine, Ten, the Math Champ Strikes Again

Carter's teacher, Mr. Snell and I finally sit down to discuss Carter's growing dislike for school. We cover all the analytical possibilities: *self-confidence, self-esteem, coping mechanisms,* etc.

I finally get up the nerve to tell him what I really think the problem is.

"I was quite taken aback by Kit's comment about Amanda's perfect math score on the state test," I say. "I really don't care about how well Amanda does. I only care about Carter."

"She shouldn't have told you that," Mr. Snell admits.

"I just think Amanda's score must have really impressed Kit, and I have a feeling that other students, like Carter, are aware of it and want to please you," I explain. "But no matter how hard they try, they can't reach the level Amanda has achieved."

This is a productive meeting as well as an honest and healthy give-and-take discussion between a teacher and a parent.

As I get up to leave, Mr. Snell gives me one last dose of perspective.

"By the way, Sasha," he says, "it might help to know that Amanda's mom was the World Champion of the International Mathematical Olympiad."

Even *I* can put two and two together!

## Update

*Carter:* Happily enjoying the third grade. She participated in dancing in the fall, softball in the spring, and is proud of herself for successfully maintaining her grade-level math score.

*Amanda:* Now doing eighth-grade math—as a third grader.

*Sasha:* When not journaling about upping the ante, pushy parents, or other potential pitfalls in Swankville, she is working on trying to solve the following math problem.

3 kids participate in 6 activities: 2 activities meet 3 times a week, 2 activities meet 1 time a week, and 1 activity meets 2 times a week. How much time during the week is left over for Sasha?

*It is a simple formula: Do your best, and somebody might like it.*

*-Dorothy Baker*

# PART II

# THEY LIVED HAPPILY EVER AFTER

"WHY DOES SHE stay in Swankville?" You may be asking yourself this question by now. Trust me, we seriously considered leaving. While visiting friends in the beautiful state of Montana last summer, we spontaneously bought our dream home. After putting down our deposit, we flew back to California and had one month to pack up our belongings and say our good-byes.

The plane ride home to Swankville was thrilling as I poured over brochures filled with hardwood floors and Italian tiles. Next to me, Eric was deep into decision-making regarding a black-bottom pool and guesthouse options. Not only was this going to be financially less stressful due to the cost of living in Montana, but it also seemed to be the perfect escape from my Swankville syndrome—or would it?

I knew I should be excited about the pink-and-green pastel tiles I just picked out for the girls' new bathroom, but within days homesickness took root in the pit of my stomach. As I drove around the streets of Swankville, my loving family and dear close friends came into focus. Suddenly, I saw only the things that made me truly happy here rather than the people and aspects of the town that had been bringing me down. I quickly came to realize that the enticing grass that's always greener probably looks that way because it's artificial.

How we raise our children isn't about the size of the home we put over their heads, the style of the car we chauffeur them in, the amount of money we spend to buy them the latest electronics, or the number of awards, trophies, and medals we help to put on their bookshelves. It is how we raise our children *in spite* of all these things. They need to be surrounded by love and feel good about emulating the first and only role models that really count—their parents.

I'm truly happy we made the decision to stay in California and be close to family. By doing so, I've learned to pay closer attention to the positive aspects of Swankville and my interactions here. The following collection of stories shows the sweeter side of Swankville. These are the moments when, as parents, we choose to do and say the right thing—in front of our children and for the sake of our children. Despite my critical eye, even I am aware and appreciative of when a Swankvillain can behave like a Swank*civil*ian.

I like people who show their true

colors.

-Bella

# CHAPTER 18

# And on Her Farm She Had Some Chickens

*5, 6 My Dog Plays with Sticks. 7, 8*
*She Just Went through the Gate. 9, 10*
*Oh No, She Has My Neighbor's Big, Fat Hens.*

"HI, SHARON, DO you mind if I pick a few of your oranges?" I call over the fence to my next-door neighbor.

"Sure, Sasha, no need to ask, especially when they're hanging over the fence into your yard," she says kindly. "By the way, we're going to get some chickens, so I hope you're okay with living next door to a small chicken farm."

Caught a bit off guard, I think to myself, *Am I okay with living next door to chickens?* Chickens in Swankville is not something I thought that I'd ever really have to consider.

The good news is that I appreciate Sharon being so kind and upfront. The even better news is that I spent many summers in Kansas with my grandparents and have great memories of wonderful vacations spent in the Midwest. I believe living next to a chicken coop will be reminiscent of those special times.

"Sharon, I really don't mind the chickens, but you should probably know that they're living next to a bird dog," I say.

I find Sharon's matter-of-fact response so refreshing. "Well, if the chickens are dumb enough to get into your yard, then they deserve whatever may come their way," she replies.

Well, fair enough! Easy peasy! No stress, no drama.

**With a cluck-cluck here and a cluck-cluck there, here a cluck, there a cluck, everywhere a cluck-cluck, Old McSasha lives next to a farm.**

Rebecca finally went back to school today after a week of fever, body aches, and vomiting, and I'm finally getting in a run today with my bird dog after a week of doctor appointments and dealing with an upstairs toilet that leaked through our downstairs ceiling. Aaahhh, time to have a moment to breathe peacefully.

I slow to a leisurely walk the last few feet back to the house. Bibbity, however, is anxious to get back to her yard. I undo her leash and watch as she races through the gate into the backyard. I slowly enter and begin to stretch my tired muscles. As I bring my head up, I glance toward the far corner of the yard and spot Bibbity crouched in full-attack mode. With her nose pointing straight ahead and her paws gripping the ground, she's got all eight of Sharon's chickens trapped right where she wants them.

I'm mortified as the chickens' wings are flapping about. I can practically see Bibbity licking her lips in anticipation of her juicy lunch.

Farm Schmarm! I'm a city girl! Who am I kidding? I don't know how to deal with chickens—unless, of course, they're shaked and baked!

Dreading a Swankvillain confrontation, I go next door and pound frantically on Sharon's door. She answers with keys and kids in hand ready to head out to the dentist's office. When I tell her the situation, she calmly follows me to the yard and begins picking the chickens up two at a time. Trying to help, without actually touching the chickens, I begin clucking my tongue and clapping my hands while politely begging the chickens to step away from the dog.

"Did the dog hurt any of them?" I ask once they have been safely removed.

"This one's wing may be a little sore, but these chicks are lucky," she says sweetly. "I better clip their wings so they can't get over the fence."

"Thank you for being so nice," I say.

"Sasha," she says, "it would be our fault if your dog got our chickens."

"Oh, thank you for being so kind," I say again as she smiles, a bit confused.

Standing on my porch, I watch as Sharon rushes off to the dentist and think to myself, *how my wonderful neighbor is not a*

*Swankvillain. She's a Swankcivilian. No, actually, she's quite simply a lovely Swan!*

"Bibbity," I say. "I've a feeling we're not in Swankville anymore."

S.B FRIED

I used to hang out with the mean girls and never felt like I belonged. After all the drama and backstabbing, it's nice to know I found my real friends.

-Emma

# CHAPTER 19

# Pat the Bunny

*Oh Wait! Not That Hard!*

"DID PATTY SEEM okay yesterday when you and Jake came by to play with him?" my friend Lynn asks, referring to her family's gray-and-white cottontail rabbit.

The concern in her furrowed brow makes my body start to tense. "Is he . . ." I pause and start again. "He isn't . . ."

"Mmhmm," she says, nodding her head. "The kids found him dead this morning when they went out to feed him."

My entire nervous system starts firing on all circuits. The familiar fear that a Swankvillain's transformation would take place right before my very eyes is almost too much to handle. Lynn is such a good person that I couldn't bear losing her to the dark side.

"Oh no! What did we do?" I start racking my brain out loud. "We just let him run on the grass. Jake picked him up a few times. Then after about twenty minutes, we put him back in his cage. He really seemed fine when we left."

"Everyone is so sad. Amy, especially, is very upset," she says, referring to her youngest daughter.

"I feel terrible," I begin. "We'll get you another bunny."

"No," says Lynn. "I'm sure you didn't do anything. It was just his time."

Wow! I didn't think she had Swankvillain blood running through her veins, but I can't always identify it before disaster strikes. Her graciousness today, however, confirms that my initial instincts were right. While I'm mentally pinching myself that I'm not just imagining her kindness, I can't help but hop on the pity pot, thinking what crappy luck I have. This reminds me of the time our other neighbors told us to help ourselves to their pool while they were out of town. We swam daily for about a week. When the husband came home early from their trip, we got a call from him asking, "Hey, did you guys swim today because the pool is flooding?" Seriously!

Fortunately, the "pool parents" are still friendly with us as I'm hoping Lynn and her family will be. Still, my confidence is a bit shaky.

The next day after Lynn let me off the hook, Becca ran upstairs to tell me that Lynn's husband, Paul, is at the door and that he wants to talk with me.

"Oh boy, here we go!" I mumble to myself as I run down the stairs ready to rumble with the paternal figure of the newly deceased bunny. He immediately stops me in my tracks.

"Sasha, you did not kill Pat," he says sincerely. "There is nothing Jake or you could have done that would have caused his death. Throughout his six years, he endured vultures rattling his cage and our own son dropping him repeatedly. Please don't worry."

My heart warms instantly as I breathe a deep sigh of relief. "Really?" I begin. "I am so grateful and relieved that you and Lynn are such true friends."

He put his arm around me and adds his final thoughts. "Lynn said you told her that you were going to buy us a new rabbit. I know you would automatically think to do something like that, and I also know how badly you feel about this unfortunate coincidence. You have such a big heart that many people take for granted. Please know that you did not kill our rabbit."

Sometimes in Swankville, good prevails. Here we have a truly dramatic, if not traumatic, situation without the drama. Sadly, a bunny died. Yet happily, a friendship survived.

I want my kids to do their best, an important distinction from being the best.

-Sasha

## CHAPTER 20

# Belle of the Ball

"MOM, I WISH I liked everything as much as I like soccer and reading," Carter confesses to me one afternoon before soccer practice.

As I lay on her bed, listening intently, I know what she is really trying to tell me. I take a deep breath and say, "Carter, if you don't like dance as much as soccer and reading, then we need to cancel your classes for this year's dance team. It's too much money and time to give up if you don't enjoy it. Aside from schoolwork and chores, you should enjoy everything as much as soccer and reading."

She looked at me sweetly with her angelic face and asks, "Will you be mad, Mom?"

I shake my head and honestly say, "I will miss seeing your cute little body in those leotards and watching your outgoing personality burst through onstage, but I want you to be doing things you want to do."

For the first few months after she stopped dancing, I'd come across a picture of her onstage with an adorable expression on her face that used to bring me such joy and feel a twinge of sadness. I wondered, a bit guiltily, if she wanted to stop dancing because she has a baby brother. I saw her interests and even her choice of clothing become a bit more tomboyish. On the other hand, I thought, perhaps, the new baby freed her to say and do what was really in her heart. Whatever the reason, the fact is that her revelation helped me take an honest look at my parenting habits.

Fortunately, I was able to catch myself and help her follow her dreams and not mine. In that moment, I discovered how easy it can be to make your child do what you want them to do and be what you want them to be. I could have easily swayed her to continue to dance when she was flat out asking for my approval to stop.

I believe Carter really did love her first year on her dance team. She would be up onstage thoroughly enjoying the moves and music. After that first year, though, I'd find myself nagging her to get her dance clothes on and making excuses to the teachers about why she wouldn't be coming to class. I never believed in pushing her to go to a class if she didn't want to. When I would ask her if she wanted to keep dancing, she always answered, "Yes." In my gut, however, I knew she was just telling me what I wanted to hear.

The same day we told her instructor that she was quitting dance happened to also be her second day of soccer practice. She began gathering her soccer equipment a full hour before practice even started. She even anxiously nagged her sister and I to get in the car well before it was time to go. Her enthusiasm was palpable.

Someone once said, "Life is like a dance. You move from one stage to another." My daughter gracefully moved to another stage, and she may move again. One thing is for certain though: No matter what stage she chooses to shine on, she will always hold the same captive audience—her parents.

Growing up, I lived in a wealthy environment though my family did not have a lot of money. This made me feel pressure to keep up even though I couldn't. The wealthier kids always had a sport to go to, an injury from the hours of multiple sports, or they studied into the night for all their As. I had to deal with the suicides, drugs, and drinking of my friends.

—Joe

## CONCLUSION

# Can't You Hear the Whistle Blowing?

M Y FRIEND GAIL pulls up in front of my house to drop Becca off from dance class and waves me over to her side of the window.

"The teacher asked the girls to perform an optional turn combo, but Becca refused even though she was asked if she wanted to do it several times," Gail explains. "I know Becca could do it, so you may want to see if something is going on with her."

As I move through the familiar routine of serving dinner and getting us all ready for bed, I drop little comments about the turn combo, hoping Becca will offer up an explanation on her own. I'm aware that I'm probably doing this as much for myself as for her—trying to quell my own uneasiness by unearthing the root of what's bothering her. She actually seems fine, but for some reason, it's eating at me that she's not doing more than just what's expected; and deep inside I know, this is now my issue.

*Use your tools, Sasha. Look in the mirror, Sasha.* Yeah, yeah. I ignore the voice of reason inside my head and hear myself nag a bit more than I should. "You know, Becca, just because you made cheer at school doesn't mean you shouldn't give your all at the dance studio," I remind her. "Your recital is only three weeks away."

*Don't shove, Sasha. Remember, just a gentle push.* I let it go and hope the right time will present itself sooner than later.

Finally, it does. "Mommy, will you snuggle me?"

I cherish these words from all my children at any age, but they are especially meaningful from a tween or teen that doesn't shower me with love all day long like the younger ones. I immediately crawl in bed beside her and simply ask, "What happened at dance today?"

In the dark of her room and the stillness of the house, she safely unleashes a torrent of words that confirm my fears. "I know I could have done that turn, but the teacher wanted it to be a tryout where some of us would make it and some would not. I just had tryouts for cheer," she says as the tears begin to flow. "It's all been so much pressure to do everything perfectly. I feel like I have to get straight As, meet new friends, make the cheerleading squad, and dance seven competitive dances." As she continues to cry it out, I just cradle her head and listen.

Remembering that it is important to do your personal best, not be the best, I tell her, "I have expectations, Becca, but I don't expect perfection."

I completely agree with everything she's saying. I knew we were overdoing it this year, especially with so many dances. As a parent, it's very difficult to always know what is right. You want to allow your child to do everything they think they want to do, but in reality, they are still the children, and we are the adults and are often required to make some of the tough decisions for them.

She continues sobbing. "So no, I really wasn't interested in learning a turn combination that is challenging for me right now."

Enough said! She is making it very clear that she has been challenged enough this year. While I have been writing about this very problem, it has been simultaneously happening under my own roof. No matter how much it hurts to admit that my daughter has been pushed too hard, which in turn is making her push herself even harder, I would be irresponsible not to pass along this very important message of stopping long enough to take a look at your child and honestly *see* him or her and then take a look at yourself and adjust your actions accordingly.

Bless her heart for working so hard and completing such an amazing year. But the key is to be able to recognize that the reason she had an amazing and successful year isn't necessarily because of all the things she *did* do; it's because of what she *didn't* do that, I believe, made it so successful:

She didn't get straight A's (she got two B's. The last time I checked, that is still pretty darn good.)

She didn't cut herself, starve herself, or harm herself in any other way that I've seen so many young girls and boys do.

Instead, she felt safe enough to talk to me, her mother. I can only hope to maintain this type of relationship with all my children. If so, my vow each day is to never shove—just give a gentle push so they will try.

Lying beside my sleeping daughter, I'm overcome with a sense of peace—if only for a tenuous moment. For in the quiet of the room, I hear in the far off distance the rhythmic sound of the train rumbling down the tracks as I have heard so many times before. Tonight, however, it reminds me of the dreaded afternoon just one year ago.

The late afternoon sun shone brightly as I watch Jake bounce joyfully around the trampoline.

He suddenly stops and points toward our back fence like he always does when he hears the train go by. "Choo-Choo, Mama!"

I had never even realized we could hear the train from our house until Jake came along to bring all of these wonderful sounds to our attention. I did feel a bit uneasy as the train seemed to be whistling more than usual.

"Choo-Choo!" the train's whistle blew loudly once, and then, again. Jake's huge grin swallows up his tiny face, and I smile right back into his sweet eyes.

*Two hours later.*

"I'm sorry I'm late," Jake's babysitter says breathlessly as she steps through the door, a bit shaken. "The cops closed down the parking lot at school because someone lay down on the railroad tracks right before school got out."

It all starts to dawn on me as she hurries to get the rest out.

"Even from inside the classroom, we could hear the train screeching on the track, trying to stop. And then the conductor blew the whistle a couple of times when he saw someone lying there."

Although I ask, I already know the answer, "It's one of the students, isn't it?"

# REALITY CHECK

# APPENDIX A

"I WAS IN FIFTH grade and had just finished watching the movie *Legally Blonde*. I immediately told my dad that I wanted to be an attorney. The very next day, he sat me down and told me how my life will need to look from here on out now that I want to be an attorney. He had a whole plan written up about how I needed to get straight As so I could get into UC Berkeley for undergrad and then on to Harvard for law school. It was as though, suddenly, there were no more options. At sixteen, I got pregnant. Now I'm a mom of a two-year-old and attending community college and working a full-time job to pay for everything. It was just too much pressure."

The above response is just one of many that I received from students in my health class that I teach at the local community college. Over the past four years, I have surveyed nearly two hundred students on their personal experiences with parental pressures while growing up.

They were all given an excerpt from a book, which had been published in the newspaper, that discusses the pressure kids are under and the lengths these kids will go in order to achieve perfection. Their essay answers are honest, enlightening, and often times, heartbreaking. While most adults understand that perfection is an unrealistic goal, children's developing brains truly believe it is a viable possibility, and they will continue to strive for it, especially if the reward is acceptance and/or love from their parents. When these kids can't get perfect grades, social recognition from the perceived "in" crowd, and/or play the best in their (or their parents) chosen sport, then they often believe they have failed and, therefore, are not worthy of their parents love and affection. Anger, depression, self-destructiveness, suicide—our kids' generation is experiencing it all.

Society pressures parents to raise perfect kids, and many of us, in turn as parents, feel like we have failed if we don't guide, shape, or mold the all-around high-achieving child. No state, county, or city is excluded.

The students surveyed have grown up in California, Oregon, Washington, Arkansas, and Montana, just to name a few. Out of 190 surveys, only 12 percent could not relate to this problem, crediting examples of positive parenting (which is covered in Part II of this book). The remaining 88 percent, however, share very compelling and personal stories. Most responses are several paragraphs in length and describe the stress that results from living in a home with very high expectations. A little more than half of the respondents had personally experienced such intense pressure that it lead to self-destructive behaviors (e.g., cutting, eating disorder, drug abuse, teen pregnancy). The remaining respondents knew a fellow student, sibling, or close friend who experienced this pressure to be perfect.

Reading the feedback from my students has been understandably troubling. However, as a mother of three children (aged two to twelve), hearing the following report from one of their school principals was downright disturbing and, ultimately, became the catalyst for this book:

"Our counseling office has had eight 5150s[1] this year alone. Three of those were sixth graders. I've been a principal at this middle school for twenty-five years, and we saw none of this until ten years ago."

—middle-school principal, Swankville, USA.

---

[1]  Section *5150* (involuntary psychiatric hold) is a section of the California Welfare and Institutions Code which allows a qualified officer or clinician to involuntarily confine a person deemed to have a mental disorder that makes them a danger to him or herself and/or others and/or gravely disabled.

# APPENDIX B

PARENTS SIGN THEIR kids up for recreational and competitive sports, extracurricular activities, and even additional academic classes with the best intentions. No doubt, they foster self-confidence, self-esteem, and self-awareness. At some point, however, the pendulum has swung too far past the positive line of centeredness, and instead, we have parents, and in turn, their children, becoming unbalanced.

Recently, my job has provided me with the fortunate opportunity to meet and work with Brandi Chastain, World Cup Soccer Champion, and Olympic Gold and Silver winner. Through the course of several conversations, she admitted that competitive sports are not what they used to be. She believes the kids' focus has changed from just wanting to have fun to wanting to be the best. Or worse, they are only participating because of pressure from their parents.

More important than her validation of what I have been feeling about the nature of parents' bad behavior, however, is her reminder of the positive reasons why we, as parents, do what we do. She confirmed that as long as a child is enjoying the sport, he or she would ultimately gain important life lessons. Parents play a large role in determining whether or not our children continue to love what they are doing.

For some reason, our generation of parents has bought into the notion that more is better, and enough is not enough. As a result, the ante is being upped. Seasonal sports are now offered and encouraged year-round by parents so their little players don't lose their edge. In the dance studio, private lessons have become the norm in order for their prima ballerina to have a leg up on the competition—that often times are very close friends.

Just as the mental and emotional toll on our children should not be ignored, neither should the physical signs of their stress. I spoke with a coach who told me of three kids on his team that are injured due to overuse—a goalie with a strained chest muscle, and two forwards who are sidelined with foot and ankle injuries. This has become the new normal, and I question what it's going to take for the pendulum to swing back to the middle.

I know it's impossible to go backward, but I have hope that, as a parent, I can put a positive foot forward. People like Brandi give me that hope as I remind myself that she is a star athlete, an Olympian nonetheless, who didn't play her chosen sport competitively until she was in high school. Let's not burn our kids out before they even make it out of middle school.

Sure, it's easier said than done, but aren't most things? For me, a first step is reminding myself of the motto and belief that I have tried to instill in my own children:

**You don't have to be the best. Just do your best.**

Perhaps this will help us all to change our thinking and, therefore, ultimately change our actions.

# AFTERWORD

MY EXPERIENCES WITH my kids in competitive sports and activities informed the backbone of *Tales From Swankville*. When I began writing out of a deep-seeded frustration, I wondered if I was being too critical in my impression of the parents around me. Was I projecting my own competitiveness onto these people? Was it that I, in my own build-up to aggressive parenting, was actually the culprit in all of this? I'm sure my friends and family had similar concerns at times.

However, as my essays became more fleshed out and I became more comfortable sharing my thoughts with a select few, I soon realized that I was clearly onto something meaningful and was tapping into a serious trend that has infiltrated my generation of parenting.

Still, I was not entirely convinced. Not until one evening, that is, when I created a test blog regarding the book and sent it to a handful of my "tried and true" friends. Unfortunately one of them leaked it and I received an email that left me devastated. It was a vitriolic rant attacking me personally and this book. The writer of this posting did not let their complete lack of information stop them from spewing anger towards the concepts and ideas that are being put forth here. Twenty-four hours later, when I picked myself up off the floor and wiped away the tears, I knew, and I mean *really* knew that I had, indeed, hit the bull's eye.

To say that this experience has been cathartic would be a gross understatement. I have looked in the mirror and changed many of my ways. Will others do the same?

## BOOK CLUB REFLECTION QUESTIONS

# *Mirror, Mirror on **Your** Wall, Have You Reflected at All?*

1. Are you able to take your share of the blame in a conflict with someone else? Would you agree that in most conflicts there are two people to blame?

2. Do you look in the mirror to see what you can do better at the end of the day? Would you agree or disagree that we can all learn from things we do well each day and things we don't do so well?

3. Do you think most people are interested in correcting their mistakes or weaknesses? Give an example of a disagreement you have had with someone when you admit your share of the blame and the other party does not. How does that feel?

4. Do you believe you or society has the biggest influence over your child's character? Why?

5. If you believe you and your spouse have the biggest influence over your children, then are you able to see the good that you model as well as the bad? Does this concern you?

6. Do you or your spouse give much thought to how your behavior may look in the eyes of your children?

7. Are you competitive with other parents?

8. Are you able to compliment other children or other parents regarding their child's success?

9. Do you give your own child compliments?

10. Do you give your own child constructive criticism?

11. Do you think you are too hard on your child?

12. Do you think you are hard enough on your child?

13. Do you give the gentle encouraging push or the too hard shove? What is an example of a gentle push versus an overbearing push? Discuss your thoughts on this issue.

14. Would you agree that some situations in life may need a bigger push to motivate a child? What is an example of a situation when a child may need a little bit more of a push than a gentle push? What would be an example of an inappropriate amount of pressure on a kid in your opinion?

15. Do you expect perfection out of your child? Why or why not?

16. If your child doesn't get the grade you think he or she deserves, do you call the teacher?

17. If your child doesn't make the team that you believe he or she should be on, do you ask questions to see how he or she may become better?

18. Have you ever tried to change a team that your child makes or change a teacher/classroom your child is placed in? Why?

19. Have you ever thought about letting life play out for your child to see what happens if life isn't fair? Do you try to intervene or save your child from life's unfairness or pain? Why or why not?

20. Do you think there could be some benefits to letting your child have some failure in life? Why or why not?

# ABOUT THE AUTHORS

**S. B. Fried** is the founder and owner of *Healthy Starts Make Healthy Hearts* (*www.creatinghealthyschools.biz.*), which is a program designed to target childhood obesity. She holds a Bachelor of Science degree in Health Science and a master's degree in Public Health with an emphasis in School and Community Health. Her experience as an educator in various settings from public health clinics to major HMO's, to her many years as a health professor at a local community college, keeps her current on trending issues for people of all ages. This is her first novel.

**Georgie H. Ikuma** is a freelance writer and editor. She holds a Bachelor of Arts degree in English and a master's degree in Communication Development with an emphasis in Professional Writing and Editing. Her experience as a writer is vast and varied from celebrity bios and feature articles, to books and marketing materials. She worked for several years in public relations for cutting-edge technology companies in the cable television industry. This is her first collaboration with S. B. Fried.

CPSIA information can be obtained at www.ICGtesting.com
Printed in the USA
LVOW100418101111

254332LV00002B/49/P